No
Ball
Games!

Susan Akass

Illustrated by Tania Hurt-Newton

RIGBY

Katy and Dad went to the wildlife park.

Katy took her new red ball with her.

"We can play with it in the park," she said.

On the way into the wildlife park they saw a sign.

It said 'No Ball Games!'

"Hold on to the ball," said Dad, "and no ball games."

First, they went to see the tiger.

The tiger wasn't growling.

The tiger wasn't playing.

He was just walking up and down, up and down, up and down his den.

He didn't have much to do.

Then, they went to see the elephants.
Katy stared at the baby elephant and the
baby elephant stared back.
"Do you like my new red ball?" asked Katy,
and she started gently bouncing her ball.

elephants

e l e p h a n

Suddenly, the baby elephant stretched out
her trunk and took Katy's ball.
"Give me back my ball!" shouted Katy.

With a snort from her trunk, the elephant
snorted the ball over the wall.

With a splash, the ball landed in the sea lions' pool.

The sea lions jumped up and played with the ball.

"Give me my ball!" shouted Katy.

Then, with a flick of his flippers, the
big sea lion flicked the ball over
the wall.

With a thud, the ball landed on the
chimpanzees' island.
Three chimpanzees played with the ball.
"Give me my ball!" shouted Katy.

One chimpanzee jumped out of a tree.
With a long, hairy arm, he threw the
ball over the lake.

With a splat, the ball landed on a muddy hippopotamus.
The hippopotamus didn't see the ball.
The ball bounced off the hippopotamus and . . .

hippopotamus

. . . landed in the farmyard corner.

"Give me my ball!" shouted Katy.

The billy goat hit the ball with
his horns and tossed it up into the air.

The ball flew through the air and
landed in the tiger's den.
It had been all over the wildlife park.

"Give me my ball!" shouted Katy.

"Grrr . . . " growled the tiger.

With a big, striped paw, the tiger pushed
the ball around his den.

Then the tiger jumped on the ball, chased it around his den, and tossed it up into the air. He was having a great time.
"You can keep my ball," said Katy.